My Wild Woolly

My Wild Woolly

Deborah J. Eaton

Illustrated by G. Brian Karas

Green Light Readers
Harcourt, Inc.
Orlando Austin New York San Diego Toronto London

"Mom," I said.
"There's a Wild Woolly in
the yard."

"Right," I said.
"He's under my bed!"

What's My

Goodness gracious me!
What animal can this be?

My animal is brow
It has four legs. It h
pointy nose. It has
fluffy tail.

A Wild Woolly is a
make-believe animal.
Can you draw a picture
of a *real* animal?

Animal?

1. Draw a picture of an animal. Do not show it to anyone!

2. Ask a friend to guess what it is. Give some clues.

Is it a fox?

Pet Peek-Over Bookmarks

The boy in the story had a Wild Woolly as a pe

What kind of pet would you like to have?

Here's a way to make a bookmark with your favorite pet peeking over the top.

You can write what you know about that pet inside!

- Fold a sheet of paper in half.

- Make the pet's face and glue it to the top.

- Open the bookmark and write what you know about the pet inside.

After you make your bookmark, you can read it to a friend!

What Do You Think?

If you could own a pet, which one would you choose?

Why?

Meet the Illustrator

G. Brian Karas enjoyed painting the pictures in this book. He has a "Wild Woolly" of his own at home—a fluffy dog named Otto!

www.HarcourtBooks.com

First Green Light Readers edition 2005
Green Light Readers is a trademark of Harcourt, Inc., registered in the United States of America and/or other jurisdictions.

Library of Congress Cataloging-in-Publication Data
Eaton, Deborah J.
My Wild Woolly/Deborah J. Eaton; illustrated by G. Brian Karas.
p. cm.
"Green Light Readers."
Summary: A boy discovers an imaginary animal in his backyard, but his mother does not believe it is there.
[1. Imaginary creatures—Fiction. 2. Play—Fiction. 3. Imagination—Fiction.]
I. Karas, Brian, ill. II. Title. III. Series: Green Light reader.
PZ7.E1338My 2005
[E]—dc22   2004021933
ISBN 0-15-205148-1
ISBN 0-15-205147-3 (pb)

C E G H F D
C E G H F D (pb)

Ages 5–7
Grade: 1
Guided Reading Level: F
Reading Recovery Level: 9–10

Green Light Readers
For the reader who's ready to GO!

"A must-have for any family with a beginning reader."—*Boston Sunday Herald*

"You can't go wrong with adding several copies of these terrific books to your beginning-to-read collection."—*School Library Journal*

"A winner for the beginner."—*Booklist*

Five Tips to Help Your Child Become a Great Reader

1. Get involved. Reading aloud to and with your child is just as important as encouraging your child to read independently.

2. Be curious. Ask questions about what your child is reading.

3. Make reading fun. Allow your child to pick books on subjects that interest her or him.

4. Words are everywhere—not just in books. Practice reading signs, packages, and cereal boxes with your child.

5. Set a good example. Make sure your child sees YOU reading.

Why Green Light Readers Is the Best Series for Your New Reader

● Created exclusively for beginning readers by some of the biggest and brightest names in children's books

● Reinforces the reading skills your child is learning in school

● Encourages children to read—and finish—books by themselves

● Offers extra enrichment through fun, age-appropriate activities unique to each story

● Incorporates characteristics of the Reading Recovery program used by educators

● Developed with Harcourt School Publishers and credentialed educational consultants